The artist gratefully acknowledges the permission granted by Maurice Sendak for the use of characters from *Where the Wild Things Are*, © 1963 by Maurice Sendak.

This paperback edition first published in 2007 by Andersen Press Ltd.
First published in Great Britain in 1986 by Andersen Press Ltd., 20 Vauxhall Bridge Road, London SW1V 2SA.
Published in Australia by Random House Australia Pty., Level 3, 100 Pacific Highway, North Sydney, NSW 2060.
Text copyright © Jeanne Willis, 1986. Illustration copyright © Susan Varley, 1986.
The rights of Jeanne Willis and Susan Varley to be identified as the author and illustrator
of this work have been asserted by them in accordance with the Copyright, Designs and Patents Act, 1988.
All rights reserved. Colour separated in Switzerland by Photolitho AG, Zürich.
Printed and bound in Italy by Grafiche AZ, Verona.

10   9   8   7   6   5   4

British Library Cataloguing in Publication Data available.

ISBN 978 1 84270 222 2

This book has been printed on acid-free paper

The MONSTER Bed

Jeanne Willis and Susan Varley

Andersen Press

Never go down to the Withering Wood,

The goblins and ghoulies are up to no good.

The gnomes are all nasty, the trolls are all hairy

And even the pixies and fairies are scary.

Oh, never go down there, unless you are brave,

In case you discover the Cobbeldy Cave.

For inside that cave which is gloomy and glum

Live Dennis the monster and Dennis's mum.

Now Dennis the monster was mostly polite;

He tried very hard not to bellow and bite,

Except, I'm afraid, when the time came for bed.

"I'm frightened! I'm frightened!" the wee monster said.

"But why?" asked his mummy. "There's nothing to fear,
I've given you teddy, the light switch is here."

"The humans will get me," cried Dennis. "They'll creep
Under my monster bed, when I'm asleep."

"Oh, no," said his mummy, "I cannot agree,
There are no human beings, what fiddle-dee-fee.
They are only in stories. They do not exist.
Now get into bed and be quiet and kissed."

But when she bent down to kiss Dennis, he chose

To fasten his fangs round her warty old nose.

He tied up his toes in a knot round her knees.

"Led go of be, Deddid, you're hurtig be, please!"

"Only," he said, "if you help with my plan."

"All right," squealed his mummy, "I will if I can."

"Please take off my pillows and blankets," he said.

"From now on, I'd rather sleep under my bed,

For if I am there and a human comes near

It won't think to look for me, safe under here."

So there Dennis lay, staring up at the springs,
Thinking of birthdays, and chocolate and things.

Now a certain small boy who played truant from school
Got lost in the wood, in the dark—little fool!

And feeling so tired he could wander no more
He stopped at the cave and he went through the door.

He saw the bare mattress, and desperate for rest
He peeled off his wellies and stripped to his vest.

He laid himself down and he shivered with fright.

He wished that his mummy could kiss him goodnight

And check that no monsters were under the bed.

But she wasn't there . . .

SO HE DID IT INSTEAD!

The End

Look out for another story about
Dennis the Monster . . .

The
MONSTER
Storm